Born to Fly

Written and Illustrated by

H.J.Hurworth

For my children, with love x

A chubby green caterpillar held onto a crisp green leaf,
Nibbling quickly,
His body moved in waves along the branch,
Slowly and wriggly.

He was enjoying the warmth of the sun on his back,
The day was fair and bright,
Suddenly something swooped past overhead,
Briefly blocking his sunlight.

A magpie bounced down further away in the meadow,
Something shiny caught her eye,
She hopped around curiously to take a look,
Then flew back into the sky.

The caterpillar noticed lots of other birds,
Swooping and looping up there,
From treetops to rooftops and back again,
Together they soared through the air.

The caterpillar watched the birds for a moment,

Gliding around so high,

It looked so fun and so free up there...

...Oh how he wished he could fly!

On he went along the branch,
A dragonfly appeared from nowhere,
Her long sleek body and transparent wings,
Camouflaged as though not there.

But when she noticed him rippling towards her,
She suddenly flapped her wings,
She hovered above him just for a moment,
Then quickly into the sky she swings!

Leaving the caterpillar to watch her for a moment,

Expertly darting in the sky,

It looked so fun and so free up there...

...Oh how he wished he could fly!

Just then he heard a loud buzzing sound,
He climbed higher up to the top,
And saw a huge furry bumblebee,
From flower to flower she would hop.

She was busy feeding from the meadow,
And collecting lots of nectar,
She seemed to be enjoying the warm sunny air,
And the caterpillar stopped to watch her.

She buzzed and buzzed all around,

And flew up into the sky,

It looked so fun and so free up there...

...Oh how he wished he could fly!

He rippled back down the branch now,
From his movement something stirred,
Red with eight black spots,
It was a friendly little ladybird.

The ladybird crawled along a green leaf,
His legs were gripping on tight,
He opened his hard shell revealing wings,
Ready to take flight.

Off he went suddenly flying away,

Leaving the caterpillar to sigh,

It looked so fun and so free up there...

...Oh how he wished he could fly!

The caterpillar nibbled on a leaf some more,
He'd try again to fly soon,
But for now he was feeling sleepy,
And he began to build a cocoon.

He spent a long time in his bed-like home,
Contemplating and having a sleep,
His desire to fly off into the sky,
Was just becoming more deep.

He was beginning to worry it wasn't meant to be,
That he was never going to fly,
He was proud to be a chunky green caterpillar,
But he wanted to have one more try.

Feeling determined he pushed his way out,
And stretched his wings open wide...

...Yes wings!

He had turned into a butterfly!

He was full of shock and pride!

He admired his bright colourful wings,

And gave them a flutter and a beat,

His desire to fly had been innate all along,

And his transformation was now complete!

So if like the caterpillar who wanted to fly,

You feel a wish deep within you,

Be proud of who you are and don't give up...

...And your dreams will soon come true!

About the Author

With a background in teaching, H.J.Hurworth writes thoughtfully in rhyme to teach important morals to children. Her colourful style of illustration will capture and inspire young minds; sparking their imagination and creativity. H.J.Hurworth's books will help to develop children's language skills and a life-long love of reading.

Follow H.J.Hurworth and find out about her upcoming books by visiting www.HJHurworth.com.

Printed in Great Britain
by Amazon